JE   Holiday

Welcome Comfort

For Quintin Hamp—
God's speed, my friend

Patricia Lee Gauch, Editor

PUFFIN BOOKS
Published by the Penguin Group
Penguin Putnam Books for Young Readers,
345 Hudson Street, New York, New York 10014, U.S.A.
Penguin Books Ltd, 80 Strand, London WC2R ORL, England
Penguin Books Australia Ltd, Ringwood, Victoria, Australia
Penguin Books Canada Ltd, 10 Alcorn Avenue, Toronto, Ontario, Canada M4V 3B2
Penguin Books (N.Z.) Ltd, 182-190 Wairau Road, Auckland 10, New Zealand

Penguin Books Ltd, Registered Offices: Harmondsworth, Middlesex, England

First published in the United States of America by Philomel Books, a division of Penguin Putnam Books for Young Readers, 1999
Published by Puffin Books, a division of Penguin Putnam Books for Young Readers, 2002

1 2 3 4 5 6 7 8 9 10

THE LIBRARY OF CONGRESS HAS CATALOGED THE PHILOMEL EDITION AS FOLLOWS:
Polacco, Patricia.
Welcome Comfort / by Patricia Polacco.
p. cm.
Summary: Welcome Comfort, a lonely foster child, is assured by his friend the school custodian that there is a Santa Claus, but he does not discover the truth until one wondrous and surprising Christmas Eve.
ISBN: 0-399-23169-2
1. Santa Claus—Juvenile fiction. [1. Santa Claus—Fiction. 2. Christmas—Fiction. 3. Foster home care—Fiction.]
I. Title.
PZ7.P75186Wg 1999 [E]—dc21 98-29558 CIP AC

Puffin Books ISBN 0-698-11965-7

Printed in the United States of America

Welcome Comfort

PATRICIA POLACCO

PUFFIN BOOKS

Quintin Hamp was a joyous man, and a common sight at Union City Elementary School, particularly when something needed "doing." You see, he was the school custodian and he scrubbed, dusted and polished every inch of that school. But more than that, he pleasured in doing things for the children. He helped them reach things from tall shelves, bandaged skinned knees, and even made sure that no one missed their bus when school was out. He loved the children, and knew each and every one by name.

One day, as Mr. Hamp was mopping the floor in the hallway, he heard the laughter of children. Usually he loved to hear their laughter, but something wasn't right this time.

"Commooon…Comfort…come-on, waddle across the play-ground!" one of the boys jeered.

"Yeah, fatso," one of the little girls chimed in.

"What kind of a name is Comfort, anyway?" They all laughed.

When the children saw Mr. Hamp, they ran away. He put his arm around the shoulder of the boy.

"I can't help that I'm fat," the boy cried.

"Me either," Mr. Hamp chuckled. "When I was a kid, I was teased, too. As I got older, it came in real handy to be…substantial." He smiled broadly. "You must be new at school. What's your name?"

"Welcome, Welcome Comfort," the boy sputtered.

"Now, if that isn't the warmest, most inviting name I've ever heard!" Mr. Hamp grinned from ear to ear. "Tell you what, if those kids keep on being mean to you, march right in here. You can help me do my chores."

For the first time Welcome smiled. "I'd like that."

As the days passed, Welcome spent more and more time with Mr. Hamp. Sometimes Mr. Hamp took him to have lunch with him and his wife, Martha, the school librarian. They lived in a sweet little house right next to the school.

Welcome learned how to tie fishing flies with Quintin and how to make birdhouses. Welcome especially loved watching Quintin carve and whittle small toys out of wood. Martha sewed a shirt for Welcome just like Quintin's.

Welcome, who moved from foster home to foster home, and who never knew his real parents, felt part of a family at long last.

One winter day, when the children were being mean, Welcome ran into the school and found Mr. Hamp. He was his round, happy self, putting up Christmas decorations and lights.

"Don't pay any mind to them. Christmas is right around the corner, Welcome." Mr. Hamp smiled.

"What's so great about Christmas?" Welcome said.

"Why, boy, Christmas is the most wondrous time of the year!"

"It never has been wondrous for me."

"What about family? What about presents, and what about Santa?"

"I don't have any family, and Santa! He's not even real."

"He's real all right," Mr. Hamp said.

"Seein' is believin'." Welcome looked sadly at the floor.

"No, child, believin' is seein'," Mr. Hamp said with a warm smile.

"I've moved around so much, even if Santa was real, he wouldn't know where to find me."

"Child, he'll find you. Maybe he hasn't come because you haven't believed hard enough," Mr. Hamp said as he gave the boy a wink.

As Christmas approached, Welcome practiced believing. He wished that he could spend Christmas with Martha and Quintin, but each Christmas Eve they went north—it was just something they did every Christmas, Quintin said. They promised to spend the day after Christmas with him.

On the morning of Christmas Eve, Welcome helped them pack their truck to leave.

"Remember what I said, kid. Believin' is seein'," Quintin called to him as they left.

Welcome watched them drive down St. Joe Road until he couldn't see them anymore.

That evening, Welcome could hear bells ringing downtown in Union City. He looked out his window and saw people scurrying about doing last-minute shopping. He missed Quintin, but he remembered his words. He was going to try to believe with all his heart that Santa would come.

That night Welcome drifted off to sleep, but he'd wake up every once in a while and say, "There really is a Santa, there really is a Santa." But Santa didn't come. The hours passed, and Santa didn't come.

But sometime deep in the night, he was awakened out of a sound sleep. He sat straight up in bed. The room was full of light. He saw a huge man standing in the center of the light at the foot of his bed. He was wearing fur and velvet, bells and holly. He had a long silky beard and his face was shiny and bright. It was Santa.

Santa laughed and it sounded like merry bells ringing, but he said nothing to the boy. He extended his hand and pulled him from his bed, then helped the boy bundle himself up, and the next thing Welcome knew they were on the roof of the house.

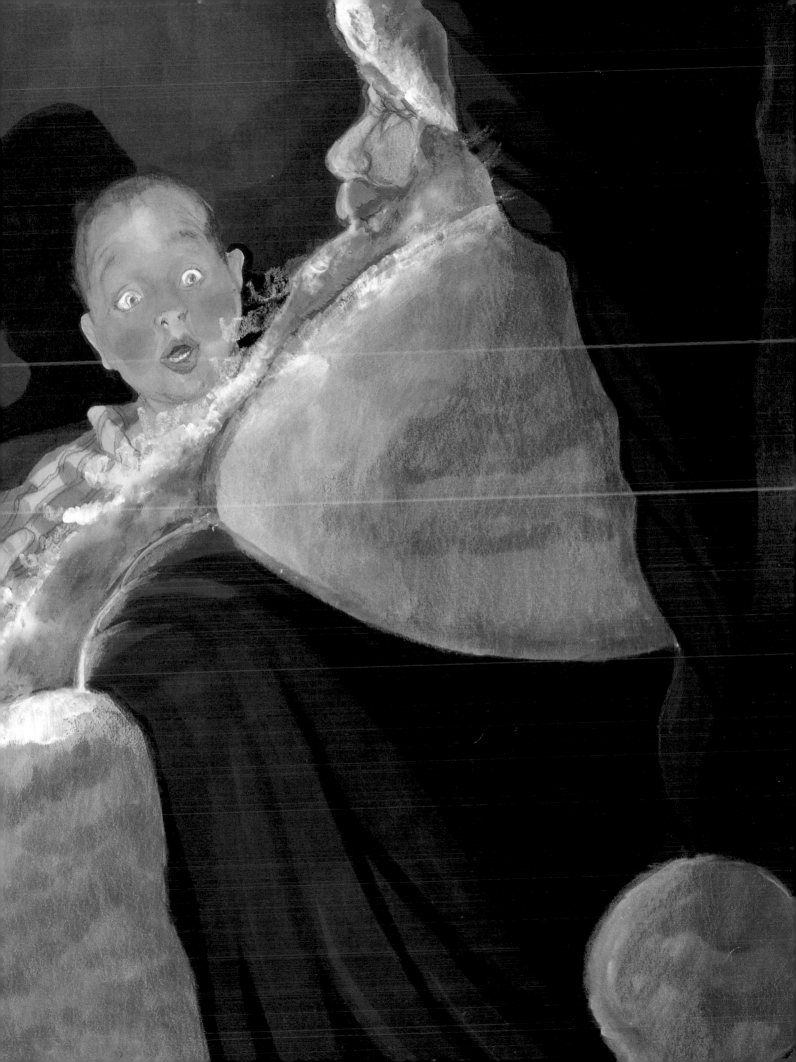

Welcome didn't even know quite how they'd gotten there. Then his eyes found a beautifully carved sleigh and stomping, snorting, sleek reindeer. Santa nudged Welcome into the sleigh and then whistled to the deer. The sleigh jerked with a start, and they were heading right for the edge of the roof.

Welcome covered his eyes. Surely they would fall over the edge! But instead, they lifted up.

All Welcome could hear was the rushing of the wind past his ears. They climbed and climbed, almost as if the sleigh were an airplane. Soon they were above the clouds, but Welcome could see the lights below. They were leaving Union City! Welcome could hardly believe what was happening.

That night, they stopped at so many places delivering trains and dolls and games and boxes of every sort that Welcome lost count. But somehow time didn't seem to pass the way it usually did. It seemed as if the night was "forever."

Soon their work was done, and they were making their long flight home. Welcome nestled into Santa's side and looked up at him.

Finally Santa spoke. "I have something for you, too, Welcome." Santa pointed at a beautiful gold pin shaped like a star that was pinned on his own vest. Behind the star was the most beautiful and perfect sprig of holly that Welcome had ever seen. "This is yours," Santa said softly.

Welcome looked at the pin as long as he could, but his eyelids got heavy, and he drifted off to sleep.

The next thing Welcome knew he was in his bed. His clothes were hung just where they always were. "Oh, no," he thought. "It was all only a dream!"

Then he remembered the pin. If Santa had really been here, the pin would be here, too. He looked everywhere—in his sheets, on the table, on the floor, but the pin was nowhere to be found.

Now Welcome knew for sure that it had all been a dream, a wonderful dream, but a dream just the same.

"How do you know that it was a dream?" Quintin asked when he and Martha came home. That was when Welcome discovered presents by the door, one of them a beautifully carved fish that Quintin had made out of wood.

"I know," Welcome said. "I know." He didn't tell them about the pin.

As the years passed, Welcome treasured that fish for many reasons. Certainly because it was the first Christmas gift from Quintin, and because it would always remind him of the Christmas of the wonderful dream.

During the next years Martha and Quintin were the next best thing to having parents. They were so proud when he graduated from high school, delighted when he got a job in the very same school where Quintin worked. They were especially happy when Welcome married a sweet girl from over Coldwater way, name of Ruby Jean.

Quintin and Welcome were always together. They fished together, carved together, and just sat and watched the sunset together. Now at the school, Welcome grew to love all of the kids almost as much as Quintin did. And Christmas became his most favored time of the year. He loved helping Quintin put decorations around the school and especially loved telling children Christmas stories.

Martha and Quintin still went up north alone for Christmas Eve— "It's just something we always do," Quintin still said—but Welcome and Ruby Jean spent every other moment of the season with them in front of their warm fireplace, there in Union City. So there was always joy at Christmastime, but Welcome could never forget the pin.

Then one year, just as Christmas vacation grew near, the principal announced that Mr. Hamp would be retiring—stepping down as Superintendent of Maintenance.

"And due to the recommendation of Mr. Hamp himself, Mr. Comfort will be taking his place." The school exploded into cheers.

"Can't think of anyone who deserves the job more than you, kid." Then Quintin added, "By the way, Martha and I want you and Ruby Jean to come up north with us this Christmas Eve."

Not only had Welcome gotten that wonderful promotion, Quintin and Martha had invited him and Ruby to be with them on Christmas Eve!

"You sure?" he asked.

"We're sure, and high time!" Quintin said with a wink.

On Christmas Eve, after driving for the longest time, they finally arrived at the dearest little cabin just on the edge of a lush forest of pine trees. They all unpacked the truck and made supper together, then nestled in front of a crackling fire. It had started to snow, and the flakes were making patterns on the windows of the cabin.

Welcome was thinking: *I want for nothing in the world*, when Quintin handed him a beautifully wrapped small box.

"Open it...open it," Martha called out.

Welcome's heart almost stopped in his chest. There, in that little box, was a beautiful gold pin—in the shape of a star, clasped around a perfect sprig of holly.

"Where did you get this?" Welcome asked breathlessly.

"Just put it on, boy," Quintin said as he grinned from ear to ear.

Welcome pinned it to his shirt. A tingle started at the tips of his toes, moved up his legs, through his heart, and burst right out of the top of his head. Why, it felt as if light was pouring right out of his skin, and he felt himself laughing. A laugh that sounded like brass bells ringing and chiming in a bell tower.

Welcome turned to look at himself in the parlor mirror. He couldn't believe what he was seeing. There before his eyes was the same specter that he had seen in his room on that magical Christmas Eve so many years ago.

It was Santa. But this time the Santa was him.

"Told you I was retiring," Quintin said as tears glistened in his kind eyes.

"I thought you meant at school," Welcome could barely say.

"I did...but I meant this, too. It's your time now, kid."

Welcome walked outside to find reindeer gathering right next to the cabin steps. Martha was bridling the deer, and Ruby Jean was pushing bags of toys and packages up onto the sled.

"Don't worry, kid, after a few times you'll know this routine like the back of your hand," Quintin said, as Welcome stepped into the sled.

They all stood and watched as the sleigh rose.

"Be merry, son. Be merry and God's speed," Quintin called up.

But the sleigh had disappeared into the night sky. All that was left was the sound of snow falling and the distant laughter of children everywhere.

Now Welcome Comfort was a joyous man, and a common sight at Union City Elementary School, particularly when something needed "doing." He loved all of the children at that school and knew each and every one of them by name.

One day, as Mr. Comfort was building new bookcases in the library, he heard the laughter of children. Usually he loved to hear their laughter, but something was different this time. Something wasn't right.

Then, he saw a group of children gathering around one small little boy...

Patricia Polacco is the author of many timeless and award-winning books for children. It is frequently her own life and memories of people around her that suggest stories to her: *Pink and Say* from her storytelling grandparents, *Thank You, Mr. Falker* from the childhood teacher who taught her to read, and *Mrs. Mack* from the unforgettable riding teacher with whom she shared summers.

For this original Christmas tale, Patricia was inspired by her friends the Hamps, whom she met in Union City, Michigan, where she now lives. Quintin Hamp, a janitor in the Union City school system, was "a glorious storyteller, a naturalist, a lover of children, and a much-adored person in the community." Though he has passed away, Patricia believes that Quintin, a Santa Claus of a man, is out there "flying somewhere in the continuum even now."

Visit Patricia Polacco at her Web site: *www.patriciapolacco.com*